Kindergarten RULES!

by Catherine Hapka
illustrated by Mike Byrne

Scholastic Inc.

ISBN 978-0-545-75840-6

Text copyright © 2014 by Catherine Hapka
Illustrations copyright © 2014 by Mike Byrne

Published by Scholastic Inc. SCHOLASTIC and associated logos are trade-marks and/or registered trademarks of Scholastic Inc.

10 9 8 7 6 5 4 3 2 1   14 15 16 17 18 19/0

Printed in the U.S.A.   40
First printing, September 2014

Ben is in kindergarten.

Ben likes school.
But there are too many rules!

"No running, Ben,"
says Ms. Green.

"But I am late!"
Ben says.

"No running," Ms. Green says.
"That is the rule."

AaBbCc Dd EeFfG

"School has too many rules,"
Ben tells Jack and Emma.

Jack

Ben

"What did you bring for show-and-tell?" Emma asks. "I have a book."

"I have something, too,"
Ben says.

Ben

Emma

10

Ben shows his toy snake, Squiggle.
"Cool!" says Jack.

"Oops," Ben says.
"What is that?" Ms. Green asks.

"No toys in school," she says.
"You have to ask first.
That is the rule."

Ms. Green makes Ben put
Squiggle in his bag.

Ben

"Sorry, Squiggle," Ben says.
"School has too many rules!"

"When I call your name, say 'here,'" says Ms. Green.

Ben

Ms. Green calls lots of names.
Ben is bored.

"Ben. *Ben.* BEN!" Ms. Green says.
Ben jumps up.
"What?" he yells.

The kids laugh.

Emma

"You have to say 'here,'" Emma says.
"That is the rule."

"Too many rules!" says Ben.

"Time for recess,"
Ms. Green says.
Ben loves recess!

Gavin does, too.
He runs to the door.
He bumps into Ben.

"Do not push, Gavin,"
Ms. Green says.
"That is the rule."

"Sorry, Ben," Gavin says.
"It's okay," Ben says.
Maybe SOME rules are okay.

"New rule, class," Ms. Green says.

"ANOTHER rule?" Ben asks.
"You will like this rule,"
Ms. Green says.

MS. GREEN'S
KINDERGARTEN RULES

Please look my way
and listen to the things I say.

Raise your hand and always ask,
before you start on any task.

Do not push,
Do not run,
but most of all...
HAVE FUN!

"Time to shake out the sillies!"
Ms. Green says.

Ms. Green skips and shakes.

The kids skip and shake, too.

The new rule is FUN!

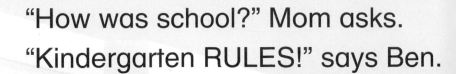

"How was school?" Mom asks.
"Kindergarten RULES!" says Ben.